Stefan Themerson

Illustrations Franciszka Themerson

THE TABLE
THAT RAN AWAY TO THE WOODS

Tate Publishing

First published in 1963 in Polish as *O stole który uciekł do lasu* by Instytut Wydawniczy 'Nasza Księgarnia' (Publishing Institute 'Our Bookshop'), Warsaw

English edition published 2012 by order of the Tate Trustees
by Tate Publishing, a division of Tate Enterprises Ltd,
Millbank, London SW1P 4RG
www.tate.org.uk/publishing

A catalogue record for this book is available from the British Library
ISBN 978 1 84976 057 7

Distributed in the United States and Canada by ABRAMS, New York
Library of Congress Control Number: applied for

Colour reproduction by Evergreen Colour Separation Co. Ltd, Hong Kong
Printed in China by Toppan Leefung Printing Ltd

Once upon a time,

THE TABLE

WHERE I WRITE

GRABBED TWO PAIRS OF SHOES,
RAN DOWNSTAIRS, AND TOOK FLIGHT,

FROM THE FIFTH FLOOR TO THE FIRST.

(ONE PAIR WAS MINE

AND THE OTHER MY WIFE'S.

IT WAS WINTER OUTSIDE
AND SLIPPERY WITH ICE.)

SO WE CHASED IT, BAREFOOT,

AND WATCHED AS IT JUMPED,

RACING INTO THE STREET,

WHERE CARS HOOTED, AND BUMPED!

THEN RIGHT OUT OF TOWN –

THROUGH FIELDS, TOWARDS TREES

IN A FOREST WHERE BRANCHES

SANG TUNES IN THE BREEZE.

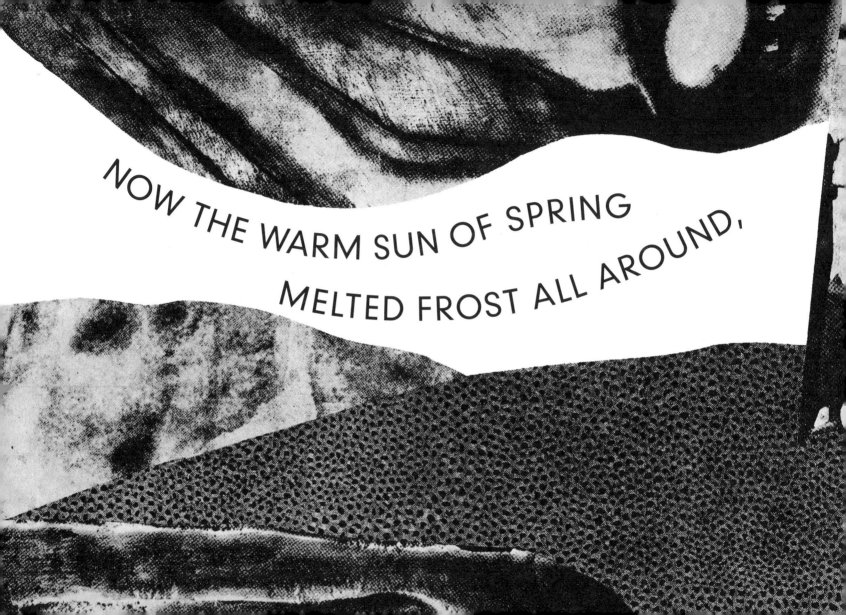

NOW THE WARM SUN OF SPRING MELTED FROST ALL AROUND,

MY TABLE STOOD STILL,

TAKING ROOT

IN THE GROUND.

AND THEN, FROM THE TABLE

WHERE INK HAD BEEN SPILLED,

A *green* LEAF SPRANG TO LIFE.

THE TABLE WAS THRILLED!

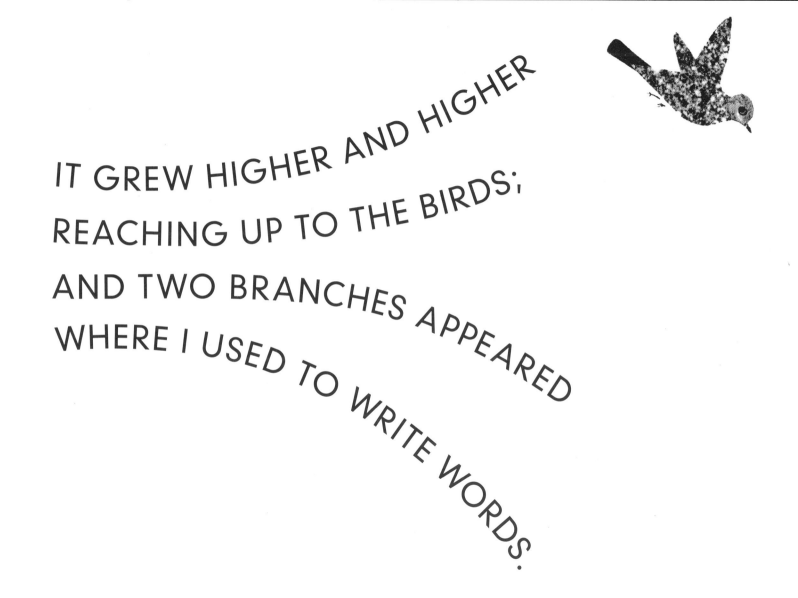

IT GREW HIGHER AND HIGHER
REACHING UP TO THE BIRDS;
AND TWO BRANCHES APPEARED
WHERE I USED TO WRITE WORDS.

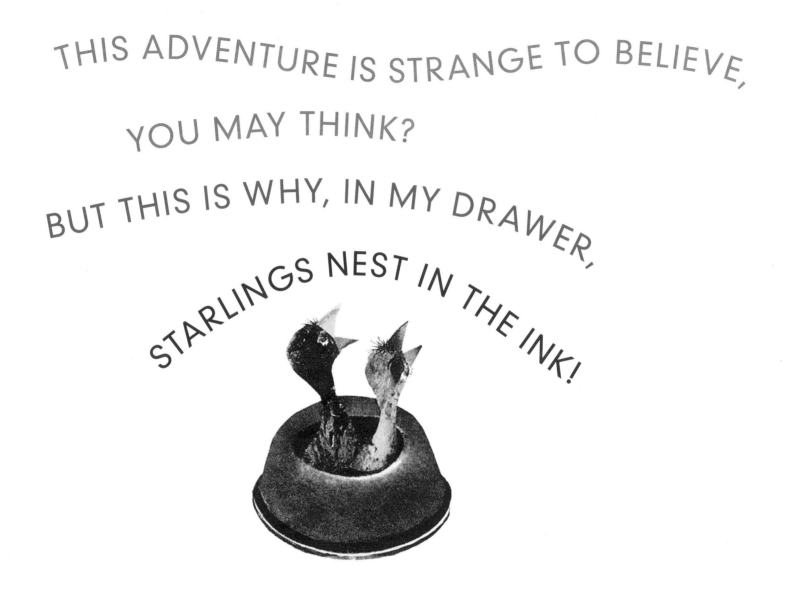

THIS ADVENTURE IS STRANGE TO BELIEVE,

YOU MAY THINK?

BUT THIS IS WHY, IN MY DRAWER,

STARLINGS NEST IN THE INK!

MOJA GAZETA   Numer 8

Opowieść o stole, który uciekł do lasu

Pewnego razu stół,
na którym piszę wiersze,
dwie pary butów wzuł
i pobiegł sobie w dół
z piątego piętra na pierwsze.

A potem ,hen, aż za miasto,
przez łąkę, przez pole i w las,
tam drzewa liściaste — iglaste
szumiały jak skrzypki i bas.

I tylko w górę rośnie
z drzewami w wyścigi mknie,
tam gdzie trzymałem łokcie
wyrosły gołęzie dwie.

To były moje buty
i mojej żony, Franciszki;
miesiąc nazywał się luty,
a luty jest zimny i śliski.

Wiosenne słońce zagrzało,
zamorza uciekał mróz,
mój stół na chwilę przystanął
i w ziemię nogami wrósł.

Na plamie z atramentu
wyrósł zielony liść,
stół bardzo jest tem przejęty
i nigdzie już nie chce iść.

Biegliśmy boso za nim,
a on — skok — susa dał
w podwórze i przez bramę
na jezdnię, z samochodami
wyścigi. Kto prędzej; W cwał!

Taka przygoda się rzadziej
niż różne inne zdarza,
lecz za to w mojej szufladzie
szpak gniazdo ma z kałamarza.

S. T.

A Note on *The Table that Ran Away to the Woods*

During the 1930s, Stefan and Franciszka Themerson were leading figures of the Polish filmmaking avant-garde in Warsaw. At the same time they published some twenty very successful books for children that he wrote and she illustrated. This pattern continued when they moved to Paris in 1938, and then to London (she in 1940, he in 1942).

The earliest published version of this delightful fable appeared in *Moja Gazeta*, the children's section of a Polish expatriate newspaper published in Paris (April 1940), illustrated with pen drawings by Franciszka (see left). It was reprinted in a slim volume of Stefan's poems *Dno Nieba*, after the Themersons were reunited in London in 1942. Sometime between those two, Stefan made an (unpublished) version in coloured lino-cuts, probably in France in 1941 or 1942 (right and overleaf).

In this story, a table escapes from the man-made urban world, out of the house, out of the town, until finally it rejoins the trees from which it originally came, and puts down roots into the soil. The spirit of the fable is very close in spirit to much of the Themersons' work of the late 1930s into the early 1940s – Franciszka's drawings and Stefan's writing. Most strikingly resonant is its similarity to the last film they made in Poland

(*Adventure of a Good Citizen*, 1938), in which a man overhears a telephone message saying that 'the sky won't fall in if you walk backwards'. Inspired, he stands up from his desk, walks gingerly backwards towards the door, and falls into two men carrying a wardrobe. He picks up one end of the wardrobe, and spends the rest of the film walking backwards, out of the city, into the woods and – like the table – back to nature. He is pursued by protesters carrying banners reading 'Forward March, Everyone! Walking Backwards is Wrong!' Finally, he flies like a bird through the wardrobe mirror and ends up sitting on rooftops playing a flute.

The symbolic role of the natural world assumed a greater poignancy in the Themersons' imagery during the war years, especially during their two years of separation, when it seemed to stand for all the lost values in a man-made world torn apart by the madness and destruction of war, when life was lived on shifting sands and in which nothing was stable or dependable or reasonable. Animals became the only sane inhabitants of the world. In Franciszka's drawings she is consoled, sitting alone at her desk, by a cow; Stefan's journey home is guided by a small dog. Stefan's wartime novel, *Professor Mmaa's Lecture*,

observes the world through the eyes of a colony of termites. The animated life of the table belongs with that world.

The 1938 film, *Adventure of a Good Citizen*, was lost during the war and only resurfaced in 1960. When someone at the Polish film archives contacted Stefan about its survival, he wrote back wondering whether the film would still seem as subversive as it had in the 1930s (several people had walked out of an early screening). It was, like the story of the table, an allegory of independence, of the individual's freedom to choose.

I think it's no coincidence that rediscovery of the film in 1960 so immediately preceded – even precipitated – publication of this radiant new collage version of *The Table that Ran Away to the Woods* (*O stole który uciekł do lasu*, Warsaw 1963), translated here for the first time. Its simple eloquence has all the innocence of a child's song, as the table dances back to nature, and the liberated typography floats across the page.

Nick Wadley